The (Almost) Totally True Story of Hansel and Gretel

Steph DeFerie

A SAMUEL FRENCH ACTING EDITION

SAMUEL FRENCH
FOUNDED 1830

SAMUELFRENCH.COM
SAMUELFRENCH-LONDON.CO.UK

FOR PRODUCTION ENQUIRIES
UNITED STATES AND CANADA
Info@SamuelFrench.com
1-866-598-8449
UNITED KINGDOM AND EUROPE
Theatre@SamuelFrench-London.co.uk
020-7255-4302

Each title is subject to availability from Samuel French, depending
upon country of performance. Please be aware that THE (ALMOST)
TOTALLY TRUE STORY OF HANSEL AND GRETEL may not be licensed
by Samuel French in your territory. Professional and amateur producers
should contact the nearest Samuel French office or licensing partner to
verify availability.

MUSIC USE NOTE

Licensees are solely responsible for obtaining formal written permission from copyright owners to use copyrighted music in the performance of this play and are strongly cautioned to do so. If no such permission is obtained by the licensee, then the licensee must use only original music that the licensee owns and controls. Licensees are solely responsible and liable for all music clearances and shall indemnify the copyright owners of the play(s) and their licensing agent, Samuel French, against any costs, expenses, losses and liabilities arising from the use of music by licensees. Please contact the appropriate music licensing authority in your territory for the rights to any incidental music.

IMPORTANT BILLING AND CREDIT REQUIREMENTS

If you have obtained performance rights to this title, please refer to your licensing agreement for important billing and credit requirements.

THE (ALMOST) TOTALLY TRUE STORY OF HANSEL AND GRETEL was originally staged by the Chatham Middle School Drama Club at the Chatham High School on Cape Cod, Massachusetts on December 9, 2011. The performance was directed by Karen McPherson, with set design by Amy Middleton and Naomi Wallace, and costume design by Betty Marshall and Melissa Marshall. Kate Owen handled lighting design, sound design, and stage management. The cast was as follows:

STREPTOCOCCUS	Alena O'Connor
SNOW WHITE	Gabby Hurley
BRUNHILDA	Hannah Novotny
MAGIC MIRROR	Cierra Capitummino
INSPECTOR WOMBAT	Seamus Sartin
SERGEANT RINGWORM	Andrew Whittle
GRETEL	Anna Terrenzi
HANSEL	Ben Garside
WILHELM	Vaughn Yerkes
LILAH	Nevaeh DeCosta
MARTA	Rachel Wallace
AMANITA PHALLOIDES	Anastasia Elmendorf
RED RIDING HOOD	Kate Paxton
WOLF	Nick Russell
PAPA BEAR	Soleil Vowell
MAMA BEAR	Ashley Simmons
BABY BEAR	Nevaeh DeCosta
FLOPSY	Emily McIlvin
PORKCHOP	Madison Beaupre
FARGO	Lucy Ryan
GOLDILOCKS	Carolyn Hanrahan
JACK	Douglas Ulrich
BLOSSOM	Alana Tucker
PRINCE CHARMING	Jan Lapinski
FLITSY	Alana Tucker

CHARACTERS

GRETEL – a little girl
STREPTOCOCCUS – a fairy godmother
SNOW WHITE – an Ogre, yes, an Ogre
HANSEL – a little boy
INSPECTOR WOMBAT – an English police inspector
SERGEANT RINGWORM – an English police sergeant
BRUNHILDA – a wicked step-mother
MAGIC MIRROR – a magical mirror
LILAH – a loving mother
WILHELM – a weak-willed father
MARTA – an evil step-mother
AMANITA PHALLOIDES – a wicked witch
LITTLE RED RIDING HOOD – a girl with treats
THE BIG BAD WOLF – a wolf who's big and bad
MOTHER BEAR – a bear
FATHER BEAR – a bear
BABY BEAR – a bear
PORK CHOP – a pig
FLOPSY – a pig
FARGO – a pig
GOLDILOCKS – a cookie seller
JACK – a poor boy who needs money
BLOSSOM – a cow
CHARMING – a prince
FLITSY – another fairy godmother

SETTING

Wherever fairy godmothers take us – on purpose
and (sometimes) by mistake...

PRODUCTION NOTE

The easiest way to stage the piece is to play everything before a drop
curtain of a forest. Small set pieces representing the woodcutter's house
(a curtain dividing the space in two), the witch's house (candy outside,
normal inside) the bear's house (outside only) should be brought on
and off as needed.

For Mrs. Drudge (who was there at the beginning)
– "Thanks, Audrey!"

(The forest. The sun is shining, the birds are singing. Lovely pastoral music plays. Ahhh…)

(a pause)

(nothing happens)

(Finally, a little girl appears at the back of the house or stage. It is **GRETEL**, *but we don't know that yet. She wears a traditional German folk dress and so looks out of place. She is also out of breath and nervously looks over her shoulder.)*

GRETEL. *(to an audience member)* 'Scuse me. Excuse me! What's going on here? *(waits for answer)* A what? A play? That's nice, that's real nice. *(casually)* I…uh… don't suppose you've seen any…oh, I don't know… policemen…around here, have you? *(waits for answer)* Good, that's good. If anyone asks, I've been here with you the whole time. Scoot over.

(GRETEL *sits in the audience.)*

(Enter **STREPTOCOCCUS**, *a fairy godmother. She has an ill-fitting dress, wings and a fairy wand.)*

STREPTOCOCCUS. *(Flitting about and waving her wand, she tugs at her dress and gives a black look to someone off.)* Hello! Hello! So sorry I'm late. There was a little problem backstage finding my dress. This isn't the right one, you can probably tell – it doesn't really fit properly here around my wings but we have to use it anyway since we can't find the right one. If only certain costume directors who shall remain nameless were more organized… Anyway, I'm here now and that's all that matters!

(She tosses a bit of glitter about.)

STREPTOCOCCUS. *(cont.)* Look at all the happy little children! Their bright and shining faces always make me feel so...

(She trips on her dress, sprains her wrist, bends her wand.)

Pickled frogs and rutabagas! *(She examines hem of dress.)* I told her this stupid thing was too long! *(She gets up.)* It's all right, I'm OK, don't get up! *(She is clearly in pain having sprained her wand-wrist but gamely carries on.)* Do you know what I am? Yes, I am a fairy godmother. My name is Streptococcus and I am full of... *(farts or burps loudly)* ...magic! *(She waves the now-damaged wand, grimaces with pain.)* Ow! Do you know why I'm here? I'm here to tell you all some lovely fairy stories of wonderment and enchantment and delightment. Doesn't that sound fabulous? Of course it does, aren't you lucky to have me. Well, then, let's begin! *(tosses glitter)* Once upon a time, there was a beautiful girl named Snow White! *(She flourishes the wand grandly, aggravating her wrist and causing her to curse in pain).* Pop-Tarts®!

*(Enter **SNOW WHITE**, an ogre.)*

*(looking at **SNOW WHITE** and shaking wand)*

What's the matter with this thing?

*(As **STREPTOCOCCUS** bangs and shakes her wand, a little boy enters from the back of the house. He is **HANSEL** but we don't know that yet. He is dressed in lederhosen and looks about.)*

GRETEL. *(standing and waving)* Psst! Pssssst! Over here!

*(**HANSEL** crosses to **GRETEL**.)*

HANSEL. What're you doing?

GRETEL. Hiding out! Look at all these kids – it's the perfect cover! Sit down! *(to audience member)* Scoot over. *(threateningly, making a fist)* He's been here the whole time, too, get me?

(HANSEL sits next to GRETEL.)

SNOW WHITE. What's wrong?

STREPTOCOCCUS. You're supposed to be Snow White.

SNOW WHITE. I am Snow White.

STREPTOCOCCUS. You're an ogre.

SNOW WHITE. An ogre named Snow White.

STREPTOCOCCUS. You're an ogre and your name is Snow White.

SNOW WHITE. A fairy godmother named after a horrible bacteria has a problem with an ogre named Snow White?

STREPTOCOCCUS. You're supposed to be a beautiful girl.

SNOW WHITE. I am a beautiful girl. *(with dignity)* A beautiful girl ogre.

STREPTOCOCCUS. This is going to be one of those days, isn't it.

SNOW WHITE. Seems like a perfectly pleasant day to me.

STREPTOCOCCUS. First the dress, now the wand…what else could possibly go wrong?

(Someone off is making a noise like an British police siren!)

*(Enter **INSPECTOR WOMBAT** and his lieutenant **SERGEANT RINGWORM**. They are English. **INSPECTOR WOMBAT** wears a trench coat and a fedora. **SERGEANT RINGWORM** wears a blue uniform with a flashing red light on top of his "Bobby" helmet, and it is he who is making the siren noise.)*

STREPTOCOCCUS. Oh, for heaven's sake!

INSPECTOR WOMBAT. Sorry to interrupt but this is a police emergency. I am Inspector Wombat of Scotland Yard and this is Sergeant Ringworm. We are very important policemen who are on the trail of two most cunning and dangerous criminals. We are professional yet friendly. Wouldn't you say so, Sergeant?

SERGEANT RINGWORM. Oh, yes, sir, very friendly indeed, sir. You've invited me over to your home on numerous occasions.

INSPECTOR WOMBAT. As I said, we are on the lookout for two most desperate and treacherous villains. Has anyone seen these children? *(He holds up a crayon drawing of two stick figures.)*

STREPTOCOCCUS. Children? The dangerous villains are children?

SNOW WHITE. That's not a very good likeness.

SERGEANT RINGWORM. The police sketch artist is sick so his five year old daughter filled in for him.

SNOW WHITE. That's very good for five.

SERGEANT RINGWORM. Isn't it? Stayed in the lines almost all the way round and everything. I particularly like the purple hair there on the boy.

STREPTOCOCCUS. There's an awful lot of children here – this could be any of them.

INSPECTOR WOMBAT. Have any of you noticed any children in the immediate vicinity acting suspiciously?

SERGEANT RINGWORM. Come now, speak up, don't be shy. Anybody seen these two kiddies mucking about?

HANSEL & GRETEL. *(looking around, pretending to look for the wanted children)* No, no, I don't see them, not around here, there must be some mistake. *(etc)*

INSPECTOR WOMBAT. Don't let the innocent faces fool you. These delinquents may be small but they are exceptionally vicious. They'd slit your throat as soon as look at you. No one is safe with them on the loose!

STREPTOCOCCUS. Inspector! You're scaring the children!

INSPECTOR WOMBAT. They should be scared. They should be very scared. Fear will keep them alive.

SERGEANT RINGWORM. You might want to dial it down a notch, sir.

INSPECTOR WOMBAT. Sorry. Sometimes my enthusiasm gets the best of me.

SERGEANT RINGWORM. Nothing to apologize for, sir. It's commendable that you feel so strongly about capturing these felons and insuring the public's well-being.

INSPECTOR WOMBAT. Nicely put, Sergeant. Thank you.

SERGEANT RINGWORM. Thank you, sir. They don't seem to be here, sir.

INSPECTOR WOMBAT. Right. Well, keep your eyes peeled, everyone. The police depend on the cooperation of you, the general public, to keep things safe for you, the general public.

SERGEANT RINGWORM. And remember that if you do spot them, do not attempt to take them into custody yourself. Rather, contact a law enforcement professional immediately.

INSPECTOR WOMBAT. Thank you and good day.

(**INSPECTOR WOMBAT** *and* **SERGEANT RINGWORM** *exit,* **SERGEANT RINGWORM** *making the siren noise again.*)

STREPTOCOCCUS Oh, that's great. Just one more thing I have to worry about. *(to* **SNOW WHITE***)* What do you want?

SNOW WHITE. You called me.

STREPTOCOCCUS. I'm afraid that was a mistake. My wand appears to be malfunctioning.

SNOW WHITE. *(disappointed)* So I came all the way over here for nothing?

STREPTOCOCCUS. I'm really very sorry…

SNOW WHITE. I can be your Snow White, you know. Just try me!

STREPTOCOCCUS. Oh, I don't think…

SNOW WHITE. Oh, please! Give me a chance, I can do it, you'll see! If you don't like the job I'm doing, I'll leave, no hard feelings. Please, please?

STREPTOCOCCUS. It's just that you're not really what I had in mind…

SNOW WHITE. *(appealing to the audience with a very sad face)* You want to let me try, don't you? You don't mind that I'm an ogre!

*(**SNOW WHITE** encourages the audience to speak up for her.)*

STREPTOCOCCUS. Oh, very well. We'll start again from the beginning. Go off over there.

*(**SNOW WHITE** exits.)*

STREPTOCOCCUS. I'm sorry, this isn't going very well, is it. And I had such high hopes...but then I was late and this horrible dress and my stupid wand and then the police interrupting and dangerous delinquents lurking about and now an ogre playing Snow White...I'm sure this isn't what you were expecting when you came here today, was it, you'll probably want your money back and I don't blame you. *(sighs)* Very well, here we go. Once upon a time, there was a beautiful girl named Snow White.

*(**SNOW WHITE** enters wearing a blond wig with a flower in it and a little short skirt.)*

She was a lovely child but her mother died and her father married an evil step-mother named Brunhilda. This woman hated the girl because everyone loved her more on account of she was so much prettier and lovelier and... *(looks at **SNOW WHITE**, shrugs)*...well, it's theatre, use your imagination.

*(Enter **BRUNHILDA**, the step-mother.)*

BRUNHILDA. *(She looks at **SNOW WHITE**, falters.)* It is true Snow White is beautiful...uh, so very, very beautiful... *(She looks to **STREPTOCOCCUS** for help.)*

STREPTOCOCCUS. *(quietly)* Just go on with it.

BRUNHILDA. But...

STREPTOCOCCUS. *(making a noise of frustrated encouragement)* Mph!

BRUNHILDA. But although she is indeed beautiful, she is certainly not as beautiful as I.

(*Enter* **MAGIC MIRROR**.)

Mirror, mirror on the wall
Who's the fairest of them all?

MIRROR. (*looking at* **SNOW WHITE**) Who's that?

BRUNHILDA. Snow White.

MIRROR. You're kidding.

BRUNHILDA. I'm not.

MIRROR. No, really, who is that?

STREPTOCOCCUS. It's Snow White! (*through gritted teeth*) Just keep going!

BRUNHILDA. Mirror, mirror, I command
Who's the fairest in the land?

MIRROR. (*looks at* **SNOW WHITE**, *looks at* **BRUNHILDA**) You are.

(**MIRROR** *turns, starts to exit.*)

BRUNHILDA. Hooray!

STREPTOCOCCUS. Wait wait wait! That's not how it's supposed to go!

MIRROR. That's how it's going *this* time.

(**MIRROR** *is almost off.*)

STREPTOCOCCUS. Get back here!

BRUNHILDA. And everyone lived happily ever after, the end!

MIRROR. Good night!

(**MIRROR** *exits.*)

STREPTOCOCCUS. Stop! You're ruining everything!

MIRROR. (*poking head in*) Oh, really? *I'm* ruining everything? You give me a Snow White that looks like that and *I'm* ruining everything?

BRUNHILDA. (*dancing around* **SNOW WHITE**) I'm the fairest in the land! I'm the fairest in the land!

(**SNOW WHITE** *looks sad.*)

STREPTOCOCCUS. *(to* **BRUNHILDA***)* No, you're not! *(to* **SNOW WHITE***)* Hang on a moment, dear, we'll get this sorted out. *(to* **BRUNHILDA** *who is still at it)* Stop that! *(to* **MIRROR***)* You! Do it right. Do it like you always do.

MIRROR. You want me to say that... *(indicating* **SNOW WHITE***)* ...that...is the fairest in the land.

STREPTOCOCCUS. Yes, I do!

MIRROR. So you want me to lie.

STREPTOCOCCUS. Yes, I do! I mean, no! I mean, not exactly. The story can't end now – it's only just started!

MIRROR. But...look at her. What else can I say?

BRUNHILDA. Leave that mirror alone! Stop bullying it! It speaks the truth and you can't change the truth to fit the situation!

STREPTOCOCCUS. *(to* **BRUNHILDA***)* Hush! *(to* **MIRROR***)* Just... be tactful. Be...kind. *(an idea!)* Remember, beauty is in the eye of the beholder. There is outer beauty...and there is inner beauty.

BRUNHILDA. Don't confuse the stupid mirror! It finally got things right for once – leave it alone! *(to* **MIRROR***)* Say one more thing and I'll smash you!

SNOW WHITE. *(sadly)* It's all right. I don't mind, really. You have to tell the truth and it's obvious she's prettier than I am. She might as well win this one time.

STREPTOCOCCUS. Mirror, mirror on the wall
Who's the fairest of them all?

MIRROR. Anyone can paint their face
To be the finest in the place.
A true, kind heart is much more rare
And valuable beyond compare.
So by that thought, you know I'm right –
The fairest one is this Snow White.

BRUNHILDA. No! You said it was me! You said I was the prettiest one this time!

STREPTOCOCCUS. But where does that leave the story?

BRUNHILDA. Who cares about the stupid old story? I have feelings too, you know. Don't *I* deserve some consideration?

STREPTOCOCCUS. But what about all the lovely children who've come to see our show?

(We hear the police siren again off.)

(Enter **INSPECTOR WOMBAT** *and* **SERGEANT RINGWORM** *as before.)*

INSPECTOR WOMBAT. Excuse me for interrupting again but Sergeant Ringworm here has alerted me to the fact that I neglected to inform you of the names of the two devious criminals that we are presently pursuing.

SERGEANT RINGWORM. Just doing my job, sir.

INSPECTOR WOMBAT. And a good job you're doing, too, Sergeant. Keep it up and I may well put you in for a commendation.

SERGEANT RINGWORM. It's nice of you to notice, sir, but there's no need to make a fuss.

INSPECTOR WOMBAT. No fuss at all, Sergeant. Dedication should be rewarded.

STREPTOCOCCUS. So what are they?

INSPECTOR WOMBAT. Hmmm?

STREPTOCOCCUS. What are their names?

INSPECTOR WOMBAT. The names of what?

SERGEANT RINGWORM. She means the villains we're after, sir.

INSPECTOR WOMBAT. Oh, yes! *(He takes out a small notebook, opens it, reads.)* The names of the two young treacherous miscreants are...Hansel and Gretel!

STREPTOCOCCUS. Well, that can't be right.

BRUNHILDA. Really? Those two innocent little kids who keep getting lost in the forest?

MIRROR. There must be a mistake.

SNOW WHITE. I don't believe it.

INSPECTOR WOMBAT. *(checking his notes again)* It says so right here – wanted for attempted murder, property damage, malicious mischief and aggravated assault with a dangerous weapon...Hansel and Gretel. I am right, aren't I, Sergeant?

SERGEANT RINGWORM. Right as rain, sir.

INSPECTOR WOMBAT. Again, sorry for the interruption. Didn't mean to spoil the fun by reminding you that two dangerous, wicked, nasty children are lurking nearby and could strike again at any moment.

SERGEANT RINGWORM. Oh, I don't think you've spoiled anything, sir.

INSPECTOR WOMBAT. Thank you, Sergeant. Afternoon, all.

(**INSPECTOR WOMBAT** *and* **SERGEANT RINGWORM** *exit as before.*)

STREPTOCOCCUS. Something's not right here.

BRUNHILDA. I don't know – I always thought those kids were a little too good to be true.

SNOW WHITE. We shouldn't judge them before we've heard their side of the story and gotten all the facts.

MIRROR. Those policemen are mixed up is all. Everyone knows Hansel and Gretel are the *victims*, not the *criminals*. Everyone's heard their story.

GRETEL. *(from her seat in the audience)* Tell it again, tell it again!

HANSEL. *(from his seat in the audience)* Yeah, tell it again! Tell us the story of Hansel and Gretel!

STREPTOCOCCUS. Sorry, we're not scheduled for that one today, I'm afraid. We're doing "Snow White."

GRETEL. But that story's all finished.

HANSEL. And we want another!

BRUNHILDA. The mirror said I'm the fairest in the land so that's it, the end. *(She puts her fingers in her ears and sings)* La la la la...I can't hear you...la la la la...I can't hear you!

MIRROR. You realize you're not going to be able to do anything else with her today.

SNOW WHITE. You may as well move on and tell another story.

HANSEL AND GRETEL. *(chanting from their seats)* We want… Hansel and Gretel! We want…Hansel and Gretel! We want…Hansel and Gretel!

STREPTOCOCCUS. Stop, stop! Even if I wanted to, I can't. We're not set up for it.

MIRROR. Can't you just use your magic wand?

SNOW WHITE. That's how she ended up with me.

MIRROR. Oh.

HANSEL. Oh, please?

GRETEL. Please, please, please?

MIRROR. Pretty please…

SNOW WHITE. …with sugar on top?

STREPTOCOCCUS. But who will play them?

HANSEL AND GRETEL. *(getting up from their seats and climbing up on the stage)* We will!

STREPTOCOCCUS. You know the story?

HANSEL. Oh, yes.

GRETEL. *Very* well.

STREPTOCOCCUS. *(to* **SNOW WHITE**, **BRUNHILDA**, **MIRROR***)* I guess we're all done with you lot, then.

BRUNHILDA. *(with her fingers still in her ears)* What?

SNOW WHITE. *(loudly, taking* **BRUNHILDA***'s fingers from her ears)* She's done with us!

BRUNHILDA. You don't have to shout.

STREPTOCOCCUS. Thank you very much, you were all marvelous, thank you.

MIRROR, SNOW WHITE, BRUNHILDA. *(exiting)* No trouble, our pleasure, let's do it again sometime…*(etc.)*

STREPTOCOCCUS. You were wonderful, Snow White. I was wrong. I'm sorry I doubted you.

SNOW WHITE. Feel free to conjure me up again anytime!

(**MIRROR, SNOW WHITE** *and* **BRUNHILDA** *exit*)

STREPTOCOCCUS. *(to* **HANSEL** *and* **GRETEL**) Now, then. Where should we start?

GRETEL. *(sweetly)* At the beginning, of course.

HANSEL. *(even more sweetly)* At "Once upon a time."

STREPTOCOCCUS. Once upon a time, there was a happy family who lived deep in the forest. *(She flourishes her wand.)* Ow! Milk Duds®!

(The wood-cutter's house is revealed. There is a main area with a fireplace or large oven containing a cooking pot. There is a smaller area separated by a hanging curtain. This is the bedroom – there are blankets and pillows.)

(Enter **LILAH** *and* **WILHELM.** **LILAH** *is wearing man's clothes and* **WILHELM** *is wearing lady's clothes. They look at each other, surprised and then look pleadingly to* **STREPTOCOCCUS.**)

STREPTOCOCCUS. *(ineffectually flourishing her wand at them to fix things)* Ow, ow, ow! Sorry, the wand's acting up today. *(to audience)* They were...

WILHELM. Wilhelm...

LILAH. ...and Lilah...

HANSEL. ...and Hansel...

GRETEL. ...and Gretel.

(**HANSEL** *and* **GRETEL** *run to* **WILHELM** *and* **LILAH** *who open their arms and hug them.*)

STREPTOCOCCUS. Wilhelm was a wood-cutter so they were as poor as church mice.

LILAH. But very happy.

(**HANSEL** *and* **GRETEL** *chase each other, shouting and laughing.*)

WILHELM. Children, children! What's gotten into you today?

LILAH. Such wild little animals I have! I'm going to have to turn you out into the forest if this keeps up.

GRETEL. Hansel pinched me and called me a wicked old witch!

LILAH. Hansel, that's not very nice!

HANSEL. I was only teasing!

LILAH. How lucky we are, my love.

WILHELM. I wish I could give you fine things, my dear. I'm afraid you made a poor bargain when you married me.

LILAH. Love is never a poor bargain.

STREPTOCOCCUS. But their happiness was not to last. One day, the mother fell ill…and died.

(**LILAH** *coughs, exits*)

STREPTOCOCCUS. The father and children were left all alone.

WILHELM. *(holding out his arms)* Oh, my poor, dear, motherless children. You are so poor and dear.

(**HANSEL** *and* **GRETEL** *run into his arms for a hug*)

HANSEL. And motherless. Don't forget motherless.

WILHELM. It's a good thing your poor, dear mother isn't here to see how sad our lives are – it would kill her.

HANSEL. Poor Mother. Poor us.

GRETEL. What's for dinner, Father?

WILHELM. I'm afraid it's corn mush again, my loves. I can't afford anything finer.

HANSEL. *(making a face, to* **GRETEL***)* Maybe you can make it into something better.

GRETEL. Nobody could make corn mush into something better.

WILHELM. Your poor, dear mother could. She could take scrips and scraps of whatever was around and turn it into the most wonderful, delicious meal you ever tasted.

HANSEL. Mmmmm, I remember.

WILHELM. Just think of her stews and sauces! I would happily eat grass and grubs if they were covered in one of Mother's special gravies.

HANSEL. Stop – you're killing me!

GRETEL. Nobody in the whole world could cook as well as her!

WILHELM. Just one piece of her soft, warm bread topped with elderberry jam would be enough to fill me up from morning to noon. *(getting an idea)* Children! I have a marvelous idea! Tomorrow, I am going into town and when I return, I shall have a wonderful surprise for you!

HANSEL. Lovely chocolate sweeties?

GRETEL. A baby sister?

HANSEL. A bag of puppies?

GRETEL. A pony?

HANSEL. A bag of ponies?

WILHELM. Better than any of those! Wait and see!

(**WILHELM** *exits*)

STREPTOCOCCUS. So Wilhelm went into town and when he returned home, he was not alone.

(Enter **WILHELM** *and* **MARTA**. **WILHELM** *is wearing man's clothing.)*

WILHELM. Children, this is your new mother!

(**HANSEL** *and* **GRETEL** *run to* **MARTA** *for a hug but she folds her arms.)*

MARTA. *Step*-mother.

WILHELM. I remembered how much better and more delicious things were when there was a woman to take charge of the house so I thought it was high time we had another.

HANSEL & GRETEL. Hooray!

(**HANSEL**, **GRETEL** *and* **WILHELM** *look at* **MARTA**. *She pointedly says nothing.)*

STREPTOCOCCUS. Unfortunately, Marta, the new mother…

MARTA. *Step*-mother.

STREPTOCOCCUS. …step-mother…was very wicked and selfish. She hated the children and looked for a way to be rid of them.

MARTA. *(to* **HANSEL** *and* **GRETEL***)* Make yourselves scarce.

(**MARTA** *turns her back and crosses away as* **HANSEL** *and* **GRETEL** *go into the bedroom and draw the curtain.)*

WILHELM. What's for dinner?

MARTA. Whatever you make, I guess.

WILHELM. But I thought *you* would…

MARTA. You thought I would *what?*

WILHELM. When I met you, you said you liked to cook!

MARTA. I do. For myself. With lots of delicious ingredients. I can't do anything with this slop! There isn't even enough here to feed a squirrel, if a squirrel would even bother to take it. *(takes a clump of fur out of the cooking pot in the fireplace)* Oh my goodness, is this a squirrel?

WILHELM. Can't you manage for just a little while? With you here to watch the children, I can travel further into the forest to cut more wood and make more money. Everything will be all right soon, you'll see.

MARTA. You'll never make enough to feed us all. Growing brats…uh, children…eat and eat and eat. You know famine is stalking the land. You and I will starve while these lumps grow fat!

WILHELM. Oh my dear, I don't think it will come to that.

MARTA. And then what will happen when you are too weak and ill to work? We're doomed, I tell you, doomed! And it's all their fault!

WILHELM. *(crying)* What can we do? What can we do?

MARTA. If you truly love these vile creatures…

WILHELM. Oh, I do, I do!

MARTA. Then, you will send them off alone into the forest.

WILHELM. Yes, of course! Wait, off alone into the forest! Why?

MARTA. Because surely some other family that's more well-off will find them and take them in.

WILHELM. Another family?

MARTA. Some other lovely idiots...uh...Mummy and Daddy...that they can leech off of...uh love and depend on.

WILHELM. Do you really believe that?

MARTA. I do. I really, really do. The nasty little things will have a much brighter future than you could ever give them and we will have a wonderful life together all alone!

WILHELM. And when things get better, we can take them back...

MARTA. I don't think so.

WILHELM. ...or perhaps we can have more children!

MARTA. Uh, probably not.

WILHELM. But perhaps.

MARTA. No.

WILHELM. Buh...

MARTA. No! Now, tomorrow we shall all go on a picnic...

WILHELM. That sounds nice.

MARTA. ...and when it is time to come home, you and I will sneak away and leave them behind.

WILHELM. That doesn't sound quite so nice.

MARTA. Just remember, it's for their own good. They'll be going to a better place. *(She laughs evilly.)*

WILHELM. *(with a sigh)* I know, I know. But, it's hard to send them away. I shall miss them terribly.

(MARTA and WILHELM continue to argue silently.)

GRETEL. Did you hear that, Hansel? Papa is going to abandon us in the forest to be eaten by wild beasts!

HANSEL. I'm beginning to think our new step-mother doesn't like us very much.

GRETEL. What shall we do? How shall we find our way home again after they leave us behind?

HANSEL. Maybe we could mark a trail somehow…

GRETEL. With what? There is nothing here.

HANSEL. Perhaps we could find something in the forest.

MARTA. Then, it's all settled.

(**MARTA** *crosses and flings the curtain open, discovering* **HANSEL** *and* **GRETEL.**)

MARTA. You two! I thought I told you to go away! What did you hear?

GRETEL. Nothing. We were playing.

MARTA. *(suspicious)* Hmmm…Time for bed.

(**EVERYONE** *lies down.* **MARTA** *and* **WILHELM** *begin to snore.*)

HANSEL. Gretel! This is our chance. Come on!

(**HANSEL** *and* **GRETEL** *get up quietly, exit the house and enter the forest.*)

There must be something here we can use.

GRETEL. How about flowers?

HANSEL. They would wither and disappear. What about these white stones?

(**HANSEL** *and* **GRETEL** *pick up several white stones and put them in their pockets.*)

GRETEL. Perfect! I have the most clever brother in the whole forest!

(**HANSEL** *and* **GRETEL** *return home, lie down, go to sleep.*)

(lights out)

STREPTOCOCCUS. Bright and early the next morning, the step-mother made an announcement.

(lights up)

(**MARTA** *is standing with a basket*)

MARTA. Children, we are all going on a lovely picnic, doesn't that sound like fun? Take this.

(MARTA *thrusts the basket at* HANSEL *and* GRETEL *who rise and take it.*)

(*with a snarl*) And don't eat anything until I say so or I'll eat *you.* (*smiling*) Now let's all go and enjoy ourselves!

(MARTA *takes* WILHELM*'s arm and they exit the house and walk about the forest.* HANSEL *and* GRETEL *follow,* GRETEL *carrying the basket,* HANSEL *secretly dropping pebbles now and again.*)

HANSEL. Look – it's working perfectly! We'll easily find our way home.

GRETEL. Hooray!

WILHELM. This looks like a nice place for…

MARTA. Far enough. (*to* HANSEL *and* GRETEL) I dare say you've never been this far into the forest before, have you.

HANSEL. No, step-mother.

GRETEL. No, step-mother.

MARTA. Perfect!

(MARTA *puts out her arm for the basket.* GRETEL *hands it to her.*)

GRETEL. Can we eat now?

MARTA. (*looking in the basket*) No! Uh…I'm afraid I forgot the uh…forks. You two stay here and your father and I will go back and get some.

HANSEL. That's all right – we don't mind if…

MARTA. We need forks!

WILHELM. Really? Are you sure?

MARTA. (*meaningfully*) We…need…forks.

WILHELM. Children, you'll be perfectly safe. We'll be right back…just as soon as we get the forks. You're going to have such wonderful lives…with wonderful new forks that will take very good care of you, much better than I ever could. Do you understand?

GRETEL. No.

HANSEL. No.

WILHELM. Be brave, my darlings. The new forks will be here soon.

MARTA. Remember, stay here until we return.

(MARTA takes WILHELM's arm, takes a few steps, turns back.)

Don't move, now.

(MARTA and WILHELM take a couple of more steps and then she turns back again.)

Be sure to stay right there. Don't follow us or anything. It could be dangerous.

HANSEL. How could it be…?

MARTA. It just could! Don't you kids ever stop asking questions?

(MARTA and WILHELM retrace their route back to the house and go inside.)

HANSEL. How long should we wait?

GRETEL. There's no hurry. Let's let her think she's won for a bit.

(HANSEL and GRETEL slowly begin tracing their way back to their bedroom where they lie down and fall asleep.)

MARTA. You see? That wasn't so bad, was it?

WILHELM. The house seems so empty without their happy, smiling faces.

MARTA. You'll feel better after a delicious dinner. I'm going to make you the best meal you've ever tasted.

WILHELM. Are you really sure they're going to be all right?

MARTA. Of course I am. Right now, they're far, far away, tucked into their new warm, little beds, snug as a bug in a rug.

(sound of snoring)

(MARTA crosses, opens the curtain and sees HANSEL and GRETEL.)

MARTA. What the...?

WILHELM. Children!

MARTA. How in the world did they find their way back? *(She finds some white pebbles on the floor next to the bed and holds them up.)* What are these white stones doing here? *(understands)* They left a trail, the sneaky little brats!

WILHELM. I'm so relieved! We'll wake them for dinner, shall we?

MARTA. There isn't going to be any dinner! Go to sleep! We're getting up early to go on another picnic tomorrow.

WILHELM. But...

MARTA. I said picnic!

(WILHELM lies down, goes to sleep. MARTA looks about, takes her blanket and pillow, draws the curtain and then lies down on the other side of it and snores.)

GRETEL. Hansel, did you hear? They're going to leave us in the forest again tomorrow.

HANSEL. Don't worry. We'll just leave another trail of pebbles to follow. Did you see the look on her face when she saw us lying here? It was wonderful!

GRETEL. But we need more pebbles.

HANSEL. The forest is full of pebbles.

(HANSEL gets up, draws the curtain, finds MARTA lying there.)

MARTA. Where are you going, Hansel?

HANSEL. Oh! Uh...I was just...uh...

GRETEL. He was sleepwalking!

MARTA. Then it's a good thing I stopped him, isn't it. It's very dangerous to go out walking in the forest alone at night. Go back to bed.

(HANSEL returns to his spot, lies down.)

GRETEL. Oh, Hansel, whatever shall we do?

HANSEL. We must think some other way to mark the path back home.

(lights out)

STREPTOCOCCUS. All night long, they thought and thought and so didn't get any sleep at all. But when morning came, they still didn't know what to do.

(lights up)

*(**MARTA** is standing with a basket.)*

MARTA. Children, we are all going on a lovely picnic again, doesn't that sound like fun? Take this.

*(**MARTA** thrusts the basket at **HANSEL** and **GRETEL** who rise and take it.)*

(with a snarl) And don't eat anything until I say so or I'll eat *you*. *(smiling)* Now let's all go and enjoy ourselves!

*(**MARTA** takes **WILHELM**'s arm and they exit the house.)*

*(**HANSEL** and **GRETEL** stay behind, looking around.)*

HANSEL. There's nothing we can use!

GRETEL. *(opening the basket)* Look! Here's a bit of old bread caught in the corner! We can toss out bits of it like we did the stones.

HANSEL. Perfect! I have the most clever sister in the whole forest!

*(**HANSEL** puts the bit of bread in his pocket.)*

WILHELM. Must we really go through this again?

MARTA. Think how happy they will be and then think of all the delicious meals I'll be able to cook for you when they're gone. Children! What are you doing?

HANSEL. Coming, step-mother!

*(**HANSEL** and **GRETEL** leave the house and cross to **MARTA** and **WILHELM**. They all walk about the forest as before but this time **HANSEL** drops bits of bread.)*

(Finally, they stop.)

MARTA. Far enough.

*(**MARTA** puts out her arm for the basket. **GRETEL** hands it to her.)*

GRETEL. May we eat now?

MARTA. *(looking in the basket)* No! Uh…I'm afraid I forgot the uh…spoons. You two stay here and your father and I will go back and get some.

HANSEL. But…

MARTA. We need spoons!

GRETEL. But…

MARTA. Don't be afraid. Why, if anything should happen to us, you can easily find your way home again… just as you did yesterday.

WILHELM. *(hugging* **HANSEL** *and* **GRETEL***)* Be brave, my angels. When the new spoons get here, they'll love you just as much as I ever did. Forget about me and do what they tell you. The new spoons will make everything all right. Do you understand?

HANSEL. No.

GRETEL. No.

MARTA. Remember, stay right here until we return.

WILHELM. I love you, my darlings!

   *(***MARTA*** *takes* **WILHELM***'s arm and drags him off)*

GRETEL. She thinks she's got us this time.

HANSEL. Let's wait a long while before going back so she really believes we're gone for good.

GRETEL. I can't wait to see her face!

   (A flock of birds flies down and eats the bread crumbs.)

GRETEL. Look at all those birds. What are they doing?

HANSEL. Hey! They're eating our bread crumbs! *(flailing his arms and running at the birds)* Get out of here, you!

   (The birds fly away.)

GRETEL. *(running about looking for the trail)* They've eaten them all! The trail back home is gone! Whatever shall we do?

HANSEL. I don't know! How can two poor, innocent, helpless children hope to survive in this wicked, wicked world?

GRETEL. We shall surely perish!

HANSEL. Let us walk as long as our strength holds out. Perhaps we shall come upon some kind forest dweller who will help us.

(GRETEL *and* HANSEL *begin to walk through the forest as frightening noises are heard.*)

GRETEL. *(alarmed)* What was that?!

HANSEL. *(also alarmed)* Don't worry – it's just the wind, probably…

GRETEL. *(frightened)* What was that?!

HANSEL. *(also frightened)* Don't be scared. We're perfectly safe, aren't we?

GRETEL. *(terrified)* What was that????!!!!!

HANSEL. *(also terrified)* I'm sure it's not a dangerous animal waiting to spring out and eat us!

(*The candy house is revealed.*)

GRETEL. *(pointing at the candy house)* What's that???!!!!!

HANSEL. *(screaming)* Aaaahhhhh!!!! Wait – it looks like a house all made of candy!

GRETEL. Hooray! We're saved!

(HANSEL *and* GRETEL *run to the house and begin eating it.*)

GRETEL. I'm starving!

HANSEL. It's the most wonderful thing I've ever tasted! Let's never leave!

(*Enter* AMANITA PHALLOIDES, *a witch, from inside the candy house.*)

AMANITA. Who's that nibbling on my house?
Could it be a little mouse?
Mice may like the sweets they've tried
But tastier treats await inside!

GRETEL. Who are you?

AMANITA. Just a poor, lonely old woman who lives here all by myself in the forest. My name is Amanita Phalloides.

I've been so hoping for some lovely children to come by and keep me company. This is my house. Do you like it?

HANSEL. *(with a full mouth)* It's heavenly!

GRETEL. I've never eaten a house before!

AMANITA. You poor dears must be terribly hungry. Why don't you come in and I'll give you a proper dinner and then you can have some more sweeties after? I've got lamb and beef and fish and soft white bread. You may stuff yourself silly.

HANSEL. I can eat an awful lot.

GRETEL. I've seen him eat his weight in griddle-cakes.

AMANITA. As much as you like, I promise. Come in, come in!

(HANSEL and GRETEL enter the candy house with AMANITA following. There is a cage with a cake in it and a large oven.)

GRETEL. My, Grandma, what a big oven you have.

AMANITA. The better to cook toothsome delicacies with, my dear. Little boy, do I see a cake in that cage?

HANSEL. *(looking into cage)* However did it get in there?

AMANITA. I left it in there to cool. I didn't want any animals to get at it.

HANSEL. It looks like the tastiest cake ever baked!

AMANITA. Then you must have it! If you crawl in and take it out for me, I'll cut you the largest slice.

(HANSEL, delighted, crawls into the cage and tucks into the cake. AMANITA suddenly slams the door shut behind him and locks it.)

AMANITA. *(laughs)* Aha! Caught you!

GRETEL. Hansel!

(GRETEL runs to the cage. While her back is turned, AMANITA slips a manacle around her ankle. The manacle is attached to a long chain which is in turn attached to the wall. Alternately, it may just be a chain connecting her wrists.)

AMANITA. Aha! Caught you both!

GRETEL. What are you doing? What do you want from us?

AMANITA. You shall be my servant. *(to* **HANSEL***)* And you shall be my dinner!

*(***AMANITA** *holds up a big key and then puts it out of* **GRETEL***'s reach.)*

GRETEL. What?!

AMANITA. I'm going to fatten him up and eat him!

GRETEL. You're a monster!

AMANITA. A *hungry* monster!

GRETEL. Hansel! Pull on the bars! Try to escape!

HANSEL. *(who hasn't been listening as the cake has his full attention)* Hmm?

AMANITA. My bars and chains are too strong for your puny muscles. You're caught, good and proper.

HANSEL. Is there any whipped cream to go with this cake?

AMANITA. Of course, my little pork chop. I'll get it for you. *(to* **GRETEL***)* Now get to work sweeping out this pig sty!

*(***AMANITA** *thrusts a broom at* **GRETEL***)*

GRETEL. Never!

*(***AMANITA** *swats* **GRETEL** *with the broom until* **GRETEL** *finally gives up.)*

GRETEL. Stop! Stop!

*(***GRETEL***, crying, takes the broom and miserably begins to sweep.)*

HANSEL. Whipped cream! Whipped cream!

AMANITA. *(looking at them delightedly)* Perfect!

*(***AMANITA** *gets food from a cupboard and hands it through the bars of the cage.* **HANSEL** *shovels it into his mouth making contented grunting noises.* **GRETEL** *continues to sweep, tearfully. She occasionally makes a grab for the key but* **AMANITA** *fends her off.)*

STREPTOCOCCUS. So the days passed with Hansel growing fatter and fatter while poor Gretel had to do all the housework – cleaning and fetching water and chopping wood and every other mean chore. Amanita, however, did all the cooking herself as her food was so magically delicious that Hansel could not keep himself from eating more and more. Then, the day came when the old witch could wait no longer.

AMANITA. Girl! Build up the fire in the oven! My stomach is empty and I will have nothing but tender, succulent boy flesh to fill me up! I must have the best spices to flavor him.

(AMANITA *goes to check her spices on a rack.* GRETEL *crosses to the cage.*)

HANSEL. Gretel! This is terrible!

GRETEL. I know, I know!

HANSEL. I haven't had my afternoon cake yet!

GRETEL. Can you think of nothing but your appetite? Didn't you hear her? She is going to eat you!

HANSEL. Oh no! So does that mean no cake?

GRETEL. If only you weren't so fat… (*finding a bone on the floor*) I have an idea! When she comes near you, poke her with this bone.

(GRETEL *hands the bone to* HANSEL. HANSEL *bites it.*)

GRETEL. Don't eat it!

HANSEL. Of course I won't eat it! (*after a moment*) It tastes terrible.

(AMANITA *turns back around.*)

AMANITA. Is the oven good and hot?

GRETEL. Are you sure you want to eat him now? He's not really very fat.

AMANITA. What are you talking about? He's been cramming food down his gullet morning, noon and night for weeks now!

GRETEL. See for yourself.

(AMANITA *crosses to the cage.* HANSEL *pokes her with the bone.*)

AMANITA. Ow! (*grabbing the bone*) What is this thin, bony thing?

GRETEL. His finger! You see how scrawny he is? There's hardly any fat on him at all. He won't be very delicious.

AMANITA. Hmmm…

GRETEL. You'd better wait a while until he's plumper.

AMANITA. Very well. I'll increase his feedings. But I won't wait forever.

HANSEL. Cake, cake, cake! Make with the cake!

(**AMANITA** *shoves more food into the cage.* **GRETEL** *makes another try for the key and fails.*)

STREPTOCOCCUS. Days went by and every time Amanita Phalloides thought about cooking Hansel, he would poke out the bone to show her how thin he still was. Gretel was very happy this was keeping him alive but she couldn't come up with any way to escape.

HANSEL. Who loves cake? I love cake! Cake, cake, cake!

STREPTOCOCCUS. All too soon, it was too late.

AMANITA. Give me your finger, boy.

(**HANSEL** *pokes out the bone.*)

AMANITA. Still so thin! What is wrong with you?

GRETEL. I guess you'll just have to keep feeding him.

AMANITA. I can't wait any longer! Be he fat or be he lean, I'll swallow him from brain to spleen! *(to* **GRETEL***)* Fire up the oven good and hot. I won't be denied any longer! Now let me see, we'll need the largest roasting pan. (*She goes to sort through the cupboard again.*)

GRETEL. Hansel! Think of something!

HANSEL. You think of something – I can only think of cake!

(**AMANITA** *kicks at* **GRETEL**.)

AMANITA. I said, fire the oven, good-for-nothing, or I'll eat you, too!

(**GRETEL** *crosses to the oven, loads wood into it.*)

(*looking at her cookbook*) Now, which recipe to use? Steaks, chops, ribs, stew? Maybe just a simple roast? My mouth is watering already. *(turning back)* How is the oven, lazy-bones?

GRETEL. I can't quite get it to catch properly.

AMANITA. Stupid girl! You're more trouble than you're worth. (**AMANITA** *crosses to the oven.*) Out of my way, out of my way!

(**AMANITA** *pushes* **GRETEL** *aside and opens the oven door.*)

This will never do! You need to stack the wood this way.

(**AMANITA** *picks up a length of wood in each hand.* **GRETEL** *rushes forward, pushes* **AMANITA** *into the oven and slams the door shut with a clang!*)

(*screaming*) Ahhhh!!

GRETEL. (*grabbing the key*) We're free! We're free!

(**GRETEL** *uses the key to free herself from her chains and then unlocks the cage.*)

HANSEL. Hooray!

GRETEL. And when we…I mean…*they* got home, the evil step-mother was dead…

HANSEL. (*coming out of the cage*)…and so we…I mean… *they*…were happily reunited with their father.

(*enter* **WILHELM**)

WILHELM. Hooray!

HANSEL, GRETEL, WILHELM, STREPTOCOCCUS. …and they all lived happily ever…

(*Again, we hear the police siren off. Enter* **INSPECTOR WOMBAT** *and* **SERGEANT RINGWORM** *as before.*)

INSPECTOR WOMBAT. Stop right there! I wouldn't finish that story if I were you!

STREPTOCOCCUS. Why ever not?

INSPECTOR WOMBAT. Because you would be wrong! Isn't that right, Sergeant?

SERGEANT RINGWORM. Yes, sir. Right as rain, sir.

STREPTOCOCCUS. What are you talking about?

SERGEANT RINGWORM. They didn't all live happily ever after after all.

INSPECTOR WOMBAT. Those two children are not the innocent tykes you take them for.

STREPTOCOCCUS. Why, they're just two little dears who came up from the audience to help me tell the story.

SERGEANT RINGWORM. Ah ha! That's where you're wrong, Miss, pardon my saying.

INSPECTOR WOMBAT. Hansel and Gretel, I arrest you in the name of the law.

STREPTOCOCCUS. I told you, they're not *really* Hansel and Gretel. They're just *pretending* to be Hansel and Gretel.

INSPECTOR WOMBAT. That's what they'd like you think, all right. I put it to you that these two are, in fact, the *real* Hansel and Gretel.

SERGEANT RINGWORM. We've been on their trail for weeks, the devious little monsters. We know exactly who they are.

INSPECTOR WOMBAT. You might as well come clean – it'll go easier for you if you do.

SERGEANT RINGWORM. Well? Go on, answer him.

STREPTOCOCCUS. Tell the truth now. Are you really Hansel and Gretel?

(**HANSEL** *and* **GRETEL** *exchange glances.*)

GRETEL. *(finally)* Yes. We are.

HANSEL. But we're innocent! We're not criminals like he says!

GRETEL. We haven't done anything wrong!

SERGEANT RINGWORM. Tell that to the poor dear you pushed in the oven.

GRETEL. She was a wicked witch!

HANSEL. She was going to eat me! It was self-defense!

INSPECTOR WOMBAT. That's your side of it. Perhaps we should be fair and tell everyone the *whole* story – what you've *really* been up to.

(*Spotlight on* **INSPECTOR WOMBAT**. *In the darkness, the others exit.* **SERGEANT RINGWORM** *remains.*)

INSPECTOR WOMBAT. *(cont.)* I don't know what lies they've been telling you but this is what we've put together from our investigations. Apparently, it all started in a simple hut in the forest.

(lights up)

There was a mother and a father and two children, a boy and a girl.

(Enter **LILAH** *and* **WILHELM**. **LILAH** *is wearing a dress.* **WILHELM** *is wearing man's clothes. They cross to their house.)*

Their names were...

WILHELM. Wilhelm...

LILAH. ...and Lilah...

HANSEL. ...and Hansel...

GRETEL. ...and Gretel.

INSPECTOR WOMBAT. No one knows why these kids were so twisted. Maybe it was a result of their mother's tragic, early death.

*(***HANSEL** *and* **GRETEL** *give* **LILAH** *a threatening glare.* **LILAH** *quickly and nervously exits.)*

SERGEANT RINGWORM. Or maybe...they were just born bad.

WILHELM. Don't worry, children. I know it's hard losing your dear mother but remember that you still have me.

GRETEL. *(sarcastically)* Oh, that's comforting. You're as useful as a rhinoceros.

HANSEL. When are you going to quit fooling around with wood-cutting and get a real job?

GRETEL. Look at this mess! We want to live in a nice place and have nice things for a change.

HANSEL. And what about a decent meal once in a while? This stuff is slop! *(He throws a bowl to the floor.)*

GRETEL. Not to mention these rags we're wearing! Do you think we like going around looking like beggars?

HANSEL. We've decided it's high time you got us a step-mother – a rich one who can take care of us in style. So go into town first thing tomorrow and get one!

GRETEL. *(making a fist)* Or else!

HANSEL. And you better not come back without one if you know what's good for you!

(Frightened, WILHELM exits.)

INSPECTOR WOMBAT. We know the poor man did indeed journey into the nearby village and vainly tried to interest a local woman into marrying him. As you can imagine, he wasn't exactly overwhelmed with interested parties. But he finally managed to find one poor woman who was new to the area and hadn't heard the stories about the children.

(Enter WILHELM and MARTA)

WILHELM. Children, look! I've brought you a wonderful new mother.

HANSEL & GRETEL. *Step*-mother.

MARTA. Hello, children. My name is Marta and I'm sure we're going to be great friends before you know it.

HANSEL. Don't hold your breath.

GRETEL. So when are we moving?

MARTA. Moving?

GRETEL. Into your nice, big house in town.

MARTA. Oh, I don't have a nice, big house in town.

(HANSEL and GRETEL turn to WILHELM with quiet menace.)

HANSEL. What did we tell you about what we wanted in a step-mother?

MARTA. But I'm a good cook and I can keep house and clean and sew…

HANSEL. Do you have a huge pile of gold coins?

MARTA. Well, no…

GRETEL. How about chests of jewels and valuable treasures?

MARTA. I'm afraid not. I'm just as poor as you are, even poorer maybe.

HANSEL AND GRETEL. Then what are you doing here?!

MARTA. I do have a heart full of love to share…

GRETEL. We live in a hovel in the forest, wear rags and are practically starving to death.

HANSEL. A heart full of love isn't going to do squat!

(MARTA *begins to whimper.*)

GRETEL. And besides that, you have bad breath and you're ugly…

HANSEL. …and you have a stupid name and I can't stand the sound of your voice…

GRETEL. …and look at your hair, are you kidding me?

HANSEL. You're just a great, big useless lump!

(MARTA *breaks down and weeps.*)

GRETEL. And now you're making such horrible noises!

HANSEL. And your nose is running in the most unattractive fashion.

GRETEL. I can't even look at you, it makes me so sick to my stomach.

(HANSEL *and* GRETEL *turn away.*)

WILHELM. There, there, my dear. I'm sure once they get to know you, they'll come to love you as much as I do.

HANSEL. *(over his shoulder)* Love her? You've only known her for what, two days?

GRETEL. *(over her shoulder)* We'll never love her.

WILHELM. I'm sure you can win them over somehow. Maybe you could cook a most delicious meal just for them.

MARTA. And we could have a lovely picnic in the forest!

WILHELM. Perfect! Children! We're going on a picnic!

(MARTA *picks up the picnic basket and holds it out to* HANSEL *and* GRETEL. *They stare at her and do not take it.* MARTA *and* WILHELM *link arms and walk out into the forest. After a moment,* **HANSEL** *and* **GRETEL** *follow sullenly.)*

SERGEANT RINGWORM. Oh, yes, there was a picnic in the forest, all right.

INSPECTOR WOMBAT. But I put it to you that the children were not abandoned there as they would have you believe. Instead, they left their father very deliberately in order to get up to the most wicked mischief.

HANSEL. Maybe we could put frogs and spiders in her bed. She'd run back to town fast enough then.

GRETEL. But she'd still be alive, wouldn't she. I think we should put poisonous toadstools in her sandwich. That would get rid of her…once and for all!

*(**HANSEL** and **GRETEL** begin searching for toadstools, wandering away from* **WILHELM** *and* **MARTA**.*)*

WILHELM. Children! Don't stray away too far. Those who wander off in the forest can easily be lost forever.

MARTA. *(quietly)* And wouldn't that be just too bad.

GRETEL. What?

MARTA. Nothing.

HANSEL. It better be nothing.

*(**HANSEL** and **GRETEL** wander off.)*

MARTA. This looks like a good spot, doesn't it?

*(**MARTA** puts down the basket and she and* **WILHELM** *look around for* **HANSEL** *and* **GRETEL**.*)*

Children?

WILHELM. Hansel? Gretel? Where are you?

MARTA. *(not at all upset)* Oh, no. They've wandered off the path. *(hopefully)* They could be in terrible danger.

WILHELM. *(hopefully)* You think? I mean, don't worry, we'll find them. Let's get a good night's sleep so we'll be able to search properly.

MARTA. Maybe we should go to the village first to find some others to help us. That should only take a couple of days.

(**MARTA** *and* **WILHELM** *begin to exit in the opposite direction.*)

WILHELM. Of course, we don't want to rush things. We want to go slow and steady so we don't make any mistakes.

(**WILHELM** *and* **MARTA** *exit.*)

(*The cottage is removed.*)

INSPECTOR WOMBAT. Indeed. When most children get lost in the woods, that's the end of 'em – they fall prey to the many dangers of the forest. But as you've seen, these two are not most children.

SERGEANT RINGWORM. My sympathies lie with anyone who crosses their path.

(*Enter* **LITTLE RED RIDING HOOD**. *She carries her own basket and sings a little tune.*)

RED. (*to the tune of "Oh Suzanna." She looks in her basket.*) "Oh my Grandma, now don't you cry for me, for I'm on my way to see you with some snacks to have with tea!" Chicken wings, licorice, Rice Krispy treats, pumpkin pie. Delicious! It's a beautiful day, my basket is stuffed with treats, Granny's house is just down the path – what could go wrong? Wait, where are the deviled eggs? (*She checks the basket again, finds the eggs.*) Phew!

(*Enter* **HANSEL** *and* **GRETEL** *opposite.*)

HANSEL. Who's that?

GRETEL. More importantly, what's in her basket?

(**HANSEL** *and* **GRETEL** *cross to* **RED**.)

HANSEL. Hello. What's your name?

RED. I'm Little Red Riding Hood. Who are you?

HANSEL. I'm Hansel and this is my sister Gretel.

GRETEL. What's in your basket?

RED. Delicious goodies for my Grandma.

GRETEL. Gosh, aren't you afraid to be walking here in the deep, dark woods all by yourself?

RED. Oh, no. As long as I stay on the path, I'm perfectly safe.

HANSEL. That basket looks awfully heavy. I'd better hold it for you.

(*HANSEL takes the basket but* **RED** *doesn't let go. They each pull on it.*)

RED. Oh, that's all right.

HANSEL. No problem at all.

RED. I got it.

HANSEL. *(forcefully)* I don't mind.

RED. I said, I got it!

HANSEL. My pleasure!

(*HANSEL gives a mighty pull and ends up with the basket.*)

GRETEL. But the woods are so full of wild animals and dangerous monsters! They could eat you up whether you're on the path or not.

RED. I've never had any trouble before. Well, I better get going – my Granny's expecting me. Can I have my basket back?

(*Another tug of war over the basket but this time,* **RED** *wins.*)

RED. See you later.

(**RED** *exits.*)

GRETEL. What a Stingy Stella!

HANSEL. *(massaging his arm muscle)* She may be stingy but she's got a heck of a grip.

GRETEL. We've got to get our hands on those goodies!

HANSEL. Good luck.

GRETEL. Maybe we could frighten her. If only we were bigger and scarier looking... *(snaps her fingers)* I got it! Run after and bring her back. Tell her I've twisted my ankle and I need help. Those goodies are as good as ours.

(**HANSEL** *exits.* **GRETEL** *lies down.*)

GRETEL. *(cont.) (loudly)* Oh, dear! I've fallen and now I'm all alone and injured! Anybody could come by and eat me up. Help, help!

(Enter the **BIG BAD WOLF.***)*

WOLF. Well, well, well. What have we here? A helpless, tasty little girl, I see. It must be my lucky day.

GRETEL. Please don't eat me!

WOLF. Give me one good reason why I shouldn't.

GRETEL. Because if you let me go, I'll tell you where you can find another, tastier girl to eat...plus her extremely delicious grandmother.

WOLF. But a girl in the paw is worth two in the bush.

GRETEL. Oh, you wouldn't want me – I'm tough and stringy. Look.

*(***GRETEL** *holds out her arm.* **WOLF** *sniffs it and gives it a big lick.)*

WOLF. Heavenly!

GRETEL. But I'm so small – I'm barely an appetizer! Think what a huge meal you'll have with a girl and her granny!

WOLF. Hmmm...all right. So just where is this delectable duo?

GRETEL. The girl will be here any minute. After you talk to her and find out where her grandmother lives, you can eat her up and then go eat her granny.

WOLF. That won't work – I can't eat anyone out here on the path. If the woodsman comes along with his big ax, I'm a sitting duck.

GRETEL. So go eat the grandmother first, dress up in her clothes and when the kid comes in, she's all yours. Easy-peasy-lemon squeezy!

WOLF. I can play with her a bit before I eat her! Wonderful! Has anyone ever told you you'd make a good wolf?

GRETEL. I get that all the time.

HANSEL. *(off)* She's right over here.

RED. *(off)* But I don't think I can do anything for her. I'm not a doctor.

GRETEL. Here she comes! Hide over there and jump out as soon as we leave.

(**WOLF** *hides.*)

(**HANSEL** *and* **RED** *enter.*)

HANSEL. She needs a woman's touch to calm her.

RED. I'm sure she'll be all right. My Granny'll be worried if I'm late.

HANSEL. It'll only take a second. Just pat her hand and reassure her.

GRETEL. Oh! Ow! I'm dying, I'm dying!

(**RED** *puts down the basket and kneels beside* **GRETEL.**)

RED. There, there. It doesn't look so bad. Actually, it doesn't look like you've hurt yourself at all.

GRETEL. *(suddenly jumping up)* So I guess I must be all right, then! *(She vigorously shakes* **RED***'s hand.)* Thanks so much for your help!

HANSEL. *(grabbing the basket)* Goodbye!

(**HANSEL** *and* **GRETEL** *run off. Confused,* **RED** *watches.*)

RED. Wait! My basket!

(**WOLF** *enters.*)

WOLF. Well, hello there, my dear. Whatever is the matter?

RED. Those two kids stole my basket of goodies!

WOLF. That's terrible! You can't trust anyone in these woods nowadays. Were they especially wonderful goodies?

RED. Oh, yes, most lip-smackingly, mouth-wateringly scrumptious. I was bringing them to my Granny. Now what'll I give her?

WOLF. Perhaps you could gather some flowers. Is your Granny's house nearby?

RED. Her cottage is just down the path a short way, right by the split oak tree.

WOLF. *(pointing)* I saw some lovely daisies just over there. If you pick some, I'm sure they'll still be beautiful and fresh by the time you get to your Granny's.

RED. What a wonderful suggestion! It's nice to know there are kind people here in the forest as well as unkind ones. Thank you, Mr. Wolf.

WOLF. It's my pleasure, my dear, all my pleasure.

RED. *(exiting)* Goodbye!

WOLF. *(wiggling his fingers at her)* Goodbye!

   *(***RED** *exits.)*

   Perfect! That will give me plenty of time to…get to know…her Granny first! I just hope her nightgown is my size!

   *(***WOLF** *howls happily and exits.)*

INSPECTOR WOMBAT. I don't think I have to tell you how *that* turned out.

   (a scream offstage)

SERGEANT RINGWORM. *(shaking his head)* Tsk, tsk, tsk. Such a shame.

INSPECTOR WOMBAT. Putting those ideas into that Wolf's head the way she did, why, Gretel as good as ate that poor grandmother herself.

SERGEANT RINGWORM. So you see what we're up against – innocent faces, deadly minds.

INSPECTOR WOMBAT. *(consulting his notebook)* According to our exhaustive investigations, the children then walked further into the deep, dark woods and came upon the Bear family.

   (Enter **MOTHER BEAR, FATHER BEAR,** *and* **BABY BEAR** *with their house. They are trying to drive away the three pigs –* **PORK CHOP, FLOPSY** *and* **FARGO.***)*

FATHER BEAR. For the last time, you can't live here!

PORK CHOP. But the Wolf is after us!

FATHER BEAR. That's not our problem!

MOTHER BEAR. I'm sorry, dears, but you must build your own houses.

PORK CHOP. They keep falling down!

FARGO. I told you we shouldn't build them out of sticks and straw.

PORK CHOP. *(bopping* **FARGO***)* What do you know about it, Fargo?

FARGO. *(bopping* **PORK CHOP***)* Apparently, more than you do, Pork Chop.

FLOPSY. What about porridge? Let's build a house out of porridge! Then we can live in it *and* eat it all at the same time!

PORK CHOP. *(bopping* **FLOPSY***)* Really, Flopsy?

FARGO. *(bopping* **FLOPSY***)* A house of porridge, Flopsy?

PORK CHOP. *(bopping* **FLOPSY***)* Are you serious, Flopsy?

PORK CHOP and **FARGO**. *(both bopping* **FLOPSY***)* You ninny!

BABY BEAR. So you're the one who keeps eating my porridge! Get 'em, Dad! Make ham sandwiches out of 'em!

(Enter **HANSEL** *and* **GRETEL**. *They hide on one side, unnoticed by the others.)*

FATHER BEAR. Look – just stay out of our house.

BABY BEAR. Rip 'em apart, Dad! Tear 'em limb from limb!

FLOPSY. *(bopping* **BABY BEAR***)* Don't tear my limbs! I need my limbs!

FATHER BEAR. *(bopping* **FLOPSY***)* Did you just bop my baby?

PORK CHOP. *(bopping* **FLOPSY***)* Did you just bop their baby?

FARGO. *(bopping* **FLOPSY***)* I know I didn't just see you doing some baby-bopping.

BABY BEAR. *(bopping* **FLOPSY***)* Don't bop the baby!

MOTHER BEAR. Dear, don't bop the pig.

BABY BEAR. *(bopping* **MOTHER BEAR***)* But I want to bop the pig!

MOTHER BEAR. Did you just bop your mother?!

FATHER BEAR. That's it! We're having pork for dinner!

(**FATHER BEAR** *reaches out to grab the* **PIGS**. *They quickly run off.*)

I swear – the next person or pig who breaks into our house, I'm going to eat them up in three bites!

BABY BEAR. *(bopping* **FATHER BEAR***)* Me, too! Me, too!

FATHER BEAR. Did you just bop your father?

MOTHER BEAR. Those pigs are a bad influence. *(bopping* **BABY BEAR***)* No more bopping! Now I'm doing it!

HANSEL and **GRETEL**. *(coming forward)* Hello.

BEARS. Hello.

MOTHER BEAR. Are you two children lost?

GRETEL. Oh, no. We're having a lovely walk in the woods.

FATHER BEAR. You're not afraid of running into wild animals who might want to eat you up?

BABY BEAR. Like maybe…*(frighteningly)*…bears?!

(*BEARS roar hugely and most menacingly.* **HANSEL** *and* **GRETEL** *roar back even more menacingly. The* **BEARS** *are most impressed.*)

FATHER BEAR. Not bad.

MOTHER BEAR. Maybe you'd like to join us? We're going for a walk, as well. We're waiting for our porridge to cool.

BABY BEAR & FATHER BEAR. Porridge – bleah!

MOTHER BEAR. Porridge is nutritious. It's very good for you.

BABY BEAR. But it tastes like poopie!

MOTHER BEAR. Junior!

FATHER BEAR. We need some meat for a change.

MOTHER BEAR. So go out and hunt some down, why don't you.

FATHER BEAR. Too much effort.

MOTHER BEAR. You just had three pigs right in front of you!

FATHER BEAR. *(an excuse)* My foot hurts.

MOTHER BEAR. You are a very lazy bear. Come along, Junior.

BABY BEAR. *(bopping* **MOTHER BEAR** *and* **FATHER BEAR***)* Bop, bop, bop!

MOTHER BEAR. *(bopping* **BABY BEAR***)* I said, no more bopping!

*(*BEARS *exit.)*

GRETEL. I liked those Bears.

HANSEL. They're big and vicious and growly. What's not to like?

GRETEL. We should come back some time and play with them. They might be able to teach us a thing or two.

HANSEL. Maybe we could invite them to our house and offer them step-mother-on-toast.

(Enter a little girl with blond curls. She is dressed in a generic "scouting" outfit – kerchief around the neck, a sash with badges, a little beanie on her curls. She pulls a little wagon piled high with boxes of cookies. We don't know it yet but it is **GOLDILOCKS***.)*

GOLDILOCKS. *(singing)* "In the good old summertime, in the good old summertime, selling cookies door to door in the good old summertime!" Would you like to buy some cookies? It's for a good cause.

GRETEL. What cause?

GOLDILOCKS. We're raising money to buy cookies for needy children who don't have any.

HANSEL. Sorry. We're pretty needy ourselves…

GRETEL. …so I guess you should just give these to us right now.

*(*HANSEL *and* GRETEL *try to grab boxes of cookies.)*

*(*GOLDILOCKS *takes a defensive stance.)*

GOLDILOCKS. I wouldn't do that if I were you! *(She points to a badge on her sash.)* See that badge? I got it for giving my troop leader sponge baths when she had two broken arms.

HANSEL. So why should that scare me?

GOLDILOCKS. Who do you think broke her arms? *(pointing to another badge)* Go ahead – try stealing my cookies – I still need my leg-breaking badge.

HANSEL. Wait! Don't hit us! We can help you!

GRETEL. *(She points to the Bears' house.)* See that house over there? The people who live in it *love* cookies. They can't get enough of 'em.

GOLDILOCKS. Really?

HANSEL. You've heard of the *candy* house, right? These people want to build a *cookie* house.

GOLDILOCKS. You don't say.

GRETEL. Oh, yeah! A whole house made out of nothing but cookies.

HANSEL. So if you go on in and wait for them, they'll probably buy all the cookies you got.

GRETEL. And they won't mind or anything because they'll be so happy to see you.

HANSEL. So just make yourself at home. Have some porridge, sit down, relax. Get good and comfy.

GRETEL. Take a nap. I'm sure one of the beds is just right.

GOLDILOCKS. I am kind of tired.

GRETEL. Pulling that wagon around all day, it's no wonder. So kick your shoes off…

HANSEL. They won't be back for a while.

GOLDILOCKS. Maybe I will. Thanks – I guess I won't break your legs. Now, go on, get outta here before I change my mind.

(**GOLDILOCKS** *begins to cross to the house.* **GRETEL** *steals a box from the wagon.*)

GRETEL. Thanks, kid.

GOLDILOCKS. The name's Goldi. Goldi-locks.

HANSEL. Good luck, Goldi!

> (**GOLDILOCKS** *exits into the house with her wagon.* **HANSEL** *and* **GRETEL** *laugh evilly.*)

INSPECTOR WOMBAT. That explains everything, doesn't it. I'm sure you've always wondered how some of these terrible events came to pass. Now you know. These two criminal masterminds have been behind them all. They manipulate, connive and twist others into carrying out their horrible, shocking plans.

> (**BEAR FAMILY** *enters, crosses into house. Bear growls off! A human roar off! Bear screams of fear and pain off! The house is removed.*)

SERGEANT RINGWORM. As they made their way through the forest, they sowed their seeds of destruction with everyone they met.

> (*Enter* **JACK** *and* **BLOSSOM**.)

JACK. Have you seen a funny little man anywhere around here?

GRETEL. Nice cow.

JACK. Her name's Blossom.

BLOSSOM. Moo.

JACK. She's the best cow. I'm going to miss her.

HANSEL. Why? Where's she going?

JACK. I have to sell her. I love her with all my heart but my mother and I need money. My name's Jack.

> (**JACK** *solemnly shakes hands with* **GRETEL** *and* **HANSEL**.)

BLOSSOM. Moo.

JACK. (*patting* **BLOSSOM**) She's such a wonderful cow.

HANSEL. You'll get a lot of gold for her, I'll bet.

JACK. Even better – I heard there's a funny little man somewhere here in the forest who has magic beans and is willing to trade them for cows.

GRETEL. You don't say.

JACK. I've been looking all over but I can't seem to find him.

HANSEL. Oh, *that* funny little man! Sorry, you're too late – we sold our cow to him a little while ago and got the last of his beans.

JACK. Darn!

HANSEL. But we were just saying that we really miss our cow so maybe we could trade you the beans for Blossom.

JACK. You'd do that? Gee, that'd be swell!

GRETEL. *(holding out the box of cookies)* Only you heard it wrong. It's not magic *beans* he gave us – it's magic *cookies.*

JACK. *(taking the box)* Really?

GRETEL. Yup – amazing magic cookies.

JACK. What makes them magic?

GRETEL. Well, um, you just plant them in the ground like you would magic beans and then…look out!

HANSEL. Stand back!

GRETEL. Get the heck out of the way!

BLOSSOM. Moo?

JACK. *(very excited)* Why?! What happens then?!

GRETEL. Well, uh…

HANSEL. Um…

(They are stumped.)

JACK. *(whispering)* Do they maybe grow…cows?

HANSEL. Cows?! Why would cookies grow…

GRETEL. Yes! That's exactly what they do! These magic cow cookies grow you lots and lots of cows!

(HANSEL and GRETEL can barely keep a straight face.)

JACK. Oh my gosh! We'll be rich! *(to BLOSSOM)* I'll be able to buy you back in no time at all.

GRETEL. But you've got to…uh… *(can't think of anything)*

HANSEL. …Sing to them! Sing to them night and day! The more you sing, the quicker they grow!

GRETEL. And the more cows you get!

JACK. I've got to get home and bury them right away! Thanks! *(JACK gives BLOSSOM a kiss.)* You be a good cow! I'll see you soon!

BLOSSOM. Moo!

(JACK exits at a run.)

HANSEL and **GRETEL**. *(waving)* Bye-bye!

BLOSSOM. *(sadly)* Moo.

(HANSEL and GRETEL burst out laughing.)

GRETEL. What an idiot! I can't believe he bought it!

HANSEL. I can just picture him burying those cookies and then sitting there *singing* to them and waiting for them to grow cows!

GRETEL. You were brilliant!

HANSEL. *You* were brilliant!

BLOSSOM. Moo?

HANSEL. So now what are we going to do with a cow?

GRETEL. I'm tired of walking through these deep, dark woods. Let's ride it!

BLOSSOM. *(panicking)* Moo!

(BLOSSOM runs off.)

SERGEANT RINGWORM. That cow was the only one to escape unscathed from those malicious little fiends, the lucky thing.

INSPECTOR WOMBAT. They next met up with one Prince Charming, poor devil.

SERGEANT RINGWORM. They broke the wretched fellow's heart.

(Enter PRINCE CHARMING carrying a glass slipper.)

PRINCE CHARMING. Fair maiden! Pray allow me to ask of you a great favor. Might I try this glass slipper upon your dainty foot?

GRETEL. Are you some kind of weirdo?

PRINCE CHARMING. No, no! Allow me to explain. My parents, the King and Queen, greatly wish me to marry so last night, I gave a magnificent ball at the palace in order to meet all the eligible young women in the kingdom.

GRETEL. And check out their feet?

PRINCE CHARMING. *(ignoring her)* I met the most wonderful girl. We talked and danced and laughed all night. I fell madly in love with her.

HANSEL. So what's the problem?

PRINCE CHARMING. She refused to tell me her name or where she lived or anything about herself and then, at midnight, she ran away.

GRETEL. Don't you get it? She's just not that into you.

PRINCE CHARMING. No! I could tell she loved me as much as I loved her. Something's wrong and I want to help her. But I have to find her first.

GRETEL. And all this has to do with my feet…how?

PRINCE CHARMING. *(holding up the glass slipper)* As she ran out, she left this glass slipper behind. I realized that all I have to do to find her is to try it on every maiden in the kingdom. The foot that fits will belong to my one true love!

(HANSEL and GRETEL exchange a look.)

HANSEL. What a delightful story!

PRINCE CHARMING. Well, they don't call me Charming for nothing.

HANSEL. It's a very clever plan – I don't see how *anything* could *possibly* go wrong.

GRETEL. Of course, if it's a matter of true love, I'd be very happy to help, your Majesty.

(GRETEL holds out her hand. PRINCE CHARMING hands her the glass slipper.)

Let's just try this bad boy on and see if I'm your mystery girl.

(**GRETEL** *drops the glass slipper. It shatters.* **PRINCE CHARMING** *is horrified and speechless.* **GRETEL** *and* **HANSEL** *are not at all upset.*)

GRETEL. *(cont.)* Awww. Now look what I did – I broke it.

HANSEL. That's a real shame.

GRETEL. I don't know what happened. It just slipped through my fingers.

HANSEL. I guess now you'll never find your one true love. Never, never, never.

GRETEL. Better luck next time.

HANSEL. Have a nice day.

(**HANSEL** *and* **GRETEL** *cross away, leaving* **PRINCE CHARMING** *to pick up the broken pieces and tearfully exit.*)

PRINCE CHARMING. My shoe…my beautiful, beautiful shoe…

INSPECTOR WOMBAT. Can you believe their heartlessness?

SERGEANT RINGWORM. Poor fellow was inconsolable.

INSPECTOR WOMBAT. And that's not all. Their trail of destruction continued wherever they went – where do you think the spindle came from that pricked poor Princess Aurora?

SERGEANT RINGWORM. As of last check, her whole kingdom is still sound asleep. You can hear the snoring for miles.

INSPECTOR WOMBAT. They gave a poison apple to Snow White's step-mother and suggested she put it to good use.

SERGEANT RINGWORM. They told the Little Mermaid how much fun it was to have legs up here on land.

INSPECTOR WOMBAT. They strung up huge nets to trap Fairy Godmothers in.

SERGEANT RINGWORM. The poor dears never knew what hit them.

INSPECTOR WOMBAT. And then, they arrived at the candy house.

(*Enter* **AMANITA** *with her candy house.*)

SERGEANT RINGWORM. It's owned by a dear, sweet, old thing who's never hurt a fly.

INSPECTOR WOMBAT. The events that occurred there were, shall we say, not exactly what you've been led to believe.

SERGEANT RINGWORM. (*shaking his fists*) Those fiends!

INSPECTOR WOMBAT. (*putting an arm on* **SERGEANT RINGWORM**'s *shoulder*) Easy, Sergeant.

HANSEL & GRETEL. A candy house!

HANSEL. I'm starving!

GRETEL. Me, too!

(**HANSEL** *and* **GRETEL** *run to the house and begin eating it.*)

AMANITA. (*coming out of the house*) Children, children! You mustn't eat my beautiful home! If you're lost and hungry, I'll be happy to give you some food inside.

HANSEL. (*with his mouth full*) We want this!

AMANITA. But if you keep on so, my house will fall down!

GRETEL. (*with her mouth full*) What do we care? It's not our house.

AMANITA. Please, please come in! The best sweets are inside!

(**HANSEL** *and* **GRETEL** *finally leave off and push past* **AMANITA** *to enter the house.*)

GRETEL. What a dump!

HANSEL. So make us something to eat already, why don't you? And make it quick!

AMANITA. Please – I'm not magic, you know – I can't make it appear out of thin air. But it won't take very long – the oven is nice and hot.

(**AMANITA** *throws a stick of wood in the oven and leaves the door open.*)

HANSEL & GRETEL. Now, now, now!

(**HANSEL** *and* **GRETEL** *begin to wreck the house – overturning the table, tossing around the firewood, throwing crockery upon the floor.*)

AMANITA. Stop it! Stop it!

(**AMANITA** *manages to push* **HANSEL** *into the cage and shuts and locks the door and holds up the key.*)

You can just stay in the dog's cage until you can behave properly.

HANSEL. *(shaking the bars)* I want out! I want out!

GRETEL. *(hitting* **AMANITA** *with the broom)* You let him out, you evil, old witch!

AMANITA. Oh! You wicked girl!

(**AMANITA** *backs away until she is directly in front of the oven*)

GRETEL. Give me that key!

(**GRETEL** *grabs the key and shoves* **AMANITA** *into the oven and slams the door.*)

AMANITA. *(screaming)* Aaaahh!

(**GRETEL** *unlocks the cage, opens it and pulls* **HANSEL** *out.*)

GRETEL. Come on!

(**GRETEL** *and* **HANSEL** *try to run off but they are stopped at every turn by the entrances of* **WILHELM**, **MARTA**, **RED**, **WOLF**, **BEARS**, **PIGS**, **GOLDILOCKS**, **JACK**, **BLOSSOM**, **PRINCE CHARMING**, **STREPTOCOCCUS** *and* **FLITSY** *[another fairy godmother].* **WOLF** *is wearing a woman's nightgown.*)

SERGEANT RINGWORM. Fortunately, Fairy Godmother Flitsy here happened to come by at that very moment and saved Amanita from being burned to death in her own oven.

INSPECTOR WOMBAT. Nothing like having a fairy godmother show up when you need one.

(FLITSY *opens the oven, brings* AMANITA *forward and waves her wand over her.*)

FLITSY. There! Good as new!

AMANITA. Thank you, Fairy Godmother!

FLITSY. It's the least I can do after everything you've been through with these awful children. And don't worry, we'll have your house fixed up again in a jiffy just as soon as they've been dealt with.

(*The crowd mutters darkly.*)

CROWD. (*variously*) Give it to them good, you said it Flitsy, let's give them a taste of their own medicine, the nasty little things…(*etc.*)

SERGEANT RINGWORM. And then Flitsy went all about the forest tracking down everyone who had been harmed by these two miscreants before they all came to see us to file a complaint. We've been on their trail ever since.

INSPECTOR WOMBAT. A trail that ends here and now.

SERGEANT RINGWORM. Naturally, they've been spreading the story that *they're* the innocent victims in all this, the little weasels.

STREPTOCOCCUS. (*to* HANSEL *and* GRETEL) Well? What have you got to say for yourselves?

HANSEL. We didn't do it!

GRETEL. We're innocent! You've got to believe us!

STREPTOCOCCUS. So *all* these good people here are lying when they say you did those things?

HANSEL & GRETEL. Yes!

CROWD. (*variously*) Don't you believe it, we're telling the truth, how dare they accuse us when they're the criminals…(*etc.*)

STREPTOCOCCUS. Hold on! I think I can get to the bottom of this. All we need is an honesty spell.

ALL EXCEPT BLOSSOM. Wait! Your wand's broken! It's not going to work right! The spell will backfire! (*etc.*)

BLOSSOM. Moo!

STREPTOCOCCUS. *(waves her wand)* "We've heard from the criminals and the sleuth, now we want to hear the truth!"

WILHELM. *(to MARTA)* That dress makes you look fat.

MARTA. *(to WILHELM)* My mother told me it was a mistake to marry you and boy, was she right.

RED. My grandmother smells like mothballs.

WOLF. I like wearing women's clothing.

FATHER BEAR. When you're not looking, I throw away my porridge and eat potato chips instead.

MOTHER BEAR. I sneak out and see other bears while you're hibernating.

BABY BEAR. I poop my diapers on purpose.

PORK CHOP. I like pork fried rice.

FARGO. I've been meeting the Big Bad Wolf for coffee.

FLOPSY. I like sitting in pudding!

GOLDILOCKS. *(flipping her hair)* This is a dye job.

JACK. I am *so* tired of living with my mother.

BLOSSOM. Moo.

PRINCE CHARMING. I really don't want to get married – I want to go backpacking through the kingdom.

FLITSY. I hate being a fairy godmother – I'd rather be a stewardess.

INSPECTOR WOMBAT. I'm wearing underwear that I embroidered myself.

SERGEANT RINGWORM. Everyone knows that *I* should be *your* boss.

ALL *except* **HANSEL, GRETEL, STREPTOCOCCUS, BLOSSOM**. Now look what you've done!

STREPTOCOCCUS. Oops! I didn't mean to cast that spell on everybody – just the accused. *(to HANSEL and GRETEL)* Well?

GRETEL. *(through gritted teeth)* It's true. We're guilty.

HANSEL. We did it. Everything they said.

GRETEL. But we're not sorry and we'd do it all over again if we could!

STREPTOCOCCUS. Take them away, Inspector. I can't stand to look at them another minute.

INSPECTOR WOMBAT. I hereby arrest you in the name of the law.

SERGEANT RINGWORM. *(putting chains on* **HANSEL** *and* **GRETEL***)* Come along, you two. We've got a nice, horrible prison cell waiting with your name on it.

FLITSY. *(to* **PRINCE CHARMING***)* Don't worry, dear. I'll mend your slipper and help you find your true love. *(to the others)* And that goes for all of you – I'll make everything right for everyone again.

ALL *except* **HANSEL**, **GRETEL**, and **BLOSSOM**. Hooray!

HANSEL. Enjoy it while you can – there isn't a prison made that can hold us!

GRETEL. We'll be back! We'll be back!

HANSEL & GRETEL. *(exiting)* You haven't seen the last of Hansel and Gretel!

(**HANSEL**, **GRETEL**, **INSPECTOR WOMBAT** *and* **SERGEANT RINGWORM** *exit.*)

STREPTOCOCCUS. That may be true but for now at least, we can all live…

EVERYONE. …happily ever after!

(curtain)

PROPERTY LIST

Fairy wand

Crayon drawing of two stick figures

Police notebook

Pillows

Blankets

A squirrel or clump of fur

White stones (packing peanuts work best)

Picnic basket

Bread crumbs (smaller packing peanuts)

A flock of birds

A cake

Various kinds of food

Key

Broom

Chains

A bone

Firewood

Dishes

Bowl

Basket of goodies

A small wagon

Boxes of cookies

Glass slipper (breakable into two pieces)

COSTUME PLOT

STREPTOCOCCUS – Bright, glittery gown, wings, tiara

SNOW WHITE – Typical character dress

BRUNHILDA – Ogre costume, blonde wig, skirt

MAGIC MIRROR – Gown or pants & shirt

INSPECTOR WOMBAT – Trench coat, fedora

SERGEANT RINGWORM – Blue British Bobbie uniform, red light on hat

GRETEL – Traditional Dirndl outfit

HANSEL – Traditional lederhosen outfit

WILHELM – Rough peasant pants & shirt

LILAH – Rough peasant dress

MARTA – Peasant dress

AMANITA PHALLOIDES – Black witch dress, pointed witch hat

RED RIDING HOOD – Blouse, skirt, red cape

WOLF – Pants, shirt, wolf accents (snout, ears, tail, etc)

PAPA BEAR - Pants, shirt, bear accents

MAMA BEAR – Dress, apron, bear accents

BABY BEAR – Onesie, bear accents

FLOPSY – Funny pants & shirt/blouse & skirt, pig accents

PORKCHOP – Colorful pants & shirt/blouse & skirt, pig accents

FARGO – Crazy pants & shirt/blouse &skirt, pig accents

GOLDILOCKS – Girl Scout-type uniform, sash, beanie

JACK – Peasant pants & shirt

BLOSSOM – Cow outfit

PRINCE CHARMING – Knickers, dress shirt, cape, crown

FLITSY – Bright glitter gown, wings, tiara

SAMUEL FRENCH STAFF

Nate Collins
President

Ken Dingledine
Director of Operations,
Vice President

Bruce Lazarus
Executive Director,
General Counsel

Rita Maté
Director of Finance

ACCOUNTING

Lori Thimsen | Director of Licensing Compliance
Nehal Kumar | Senior Accounting Associate
Charles Graytok | Accounting and Finance Manager
Glenn Halcomb | Royalty Administration
Jessica Zheng | Accounts Receivable
Andy Lian | Accounts Payable
Charlie Sou | Accounting Associate
Joann Mannello | Orders Administrator

BUSINESS AFFAIRS

Caitlin Bartow | Assistant to the Executive Director

CORPORATE COMMUNICATIONS

Abbie Van Nostrand | Director of Corporate
Communications

CUSTOMER SERVICE AND LICENSING

Brad Lohrenz | Director of Licensing Development
Laura Lindson | Licensing Services Manager
Kim Rogers | Theatrical Specialist
Matthew Akers | Theatrical Specialist
Ashley Byrne | Theatrical Specialist
Jennifer Carter | Theatrical Specialist
Annette Storckman | Theatrical Specialist
Julia Izumi | Theatrical Specialist
Sarah Weber | Theatrical Specialist
Nicholas Dawson | Theatrical Specialist
David Kimple | Theatrical Specialist
Ryan McLeod | Theatrical Specialist
Carly Erickson | Theatrical Specialist

EDITORIAL

Amy Rose Marsh | Literary Manager
Ben Coleman | Literary Associate

MARKETING

Ryan Pointer | Marketing Manager
Courtney Kochuba | Marketing Associate
Chris Kam | Marketing Associate

PUBLICATIONS AND PRODUCT DEVELOPMENT

David Geer | Publications Manager
Tyler Mullen | Publications Associate
Derek P. Hassler | Musical Products Coordinator
Zachary Orts | Musical Materials Coordinator

OPERATIONS

Casey McLain | Operations Supervisor
Elizabeth Minski | Office Coordinator, Reception
Coryn Carson | Office Coordinator, Reception

SAMUEL FRENCH BOOKSHOP (LOS ANGELES)

Joyce Mehess | Bookstore Manager
Cory DeLair | Bookstore Buyer
Kristen Springer | Customer Service Manager
Tim Coultas | Bookstore Associate
Bryan Jansyn | Bookstore Associate
Alfred Contreras | Shipping & Receiving

LONDON OFFICE

Anne-Marie Ashman | Accounts Assistant
Felicity Barks | Rights & Contracts Associate
Steve Blacker | Bookshop Associate
David Bray | Customer Services Associate
Robert Cooke | Assistant Buyer
Stephanie Dawson | Amateur Licensing Associate
Simon Ellison | Retail Sales Manager
Robert Hamilton | Amateur Licensing Associate
Peter Langdon | Marketing Manager
Louise Mappley | Amateur Licensing Associate
James Nicolau | Despatch Associate
Emma Anacootee-Parmar | Production/Editorial
Controller
Martin Phillips | Librarian
Panos Panayi | Company Accountant
Zubayed Rahman | Despatch Associate
Steve Sanderson | Royalty Administration Supervisor
Douglas Schatz | Acting Executive Director
Roger Sheppard | I.T. Manager
Debbie Simmons | Licensing Sales Team Leader
Peter Smith | Amateur Licensing Associate
Garry Spratley | Customer Service Manager
David Webster | UK Operations Director
Sarah Wolf | Rights Director